P9-EGC-145

Happy Birthday,
Dear Duck

For Gregory
—J. B.

Happy Birthday
Dear Anna Eve
—E. B.

Clarion Books
Ticknor & Fields, a Houghton Mifflin Company

Printed in Italy.

Illustration backgrounds airbrushed by Joseph Hearne.

Library of Congress Cataloging-in-Publication Data
Bunting, Eve, 1928-
Happy birthday dear duck.
Summary: Duck's birthday gifts from his animal
friends are wonderful but cannot be used away from
the water, a problem eventually solved by the arrival
of his last gift.
[1. Ducks—Fiction. 2. Animals—Fiction.
3. Gifts—Fiction. 4. Birthdays—Fiction]
I. Brett, Jan, 1949- ill. II. Title.
PZ7.B91527Han 1988 [E] 87-156
ISBN 0-89919-541-5

NI 10 9 8 7 6 5 4 3 2 1

Happy Birthday, Dear Duck

by Eve Bunting

illustrated by Jan Brett

Clarion Books
TICKNOR & FIELDS: A HOUGHTON MIFFLIN COMPANY
New York

For his birthday, Duck got a swimming suit
Striped red and blue
With a hole for his tail to come through.

For his birthday, Duck got a big, green hat
With braid round the brim.
It looked good on him.

For his birthday, Duck got a fat, yellow chair
The kind you can float in.
Or play you're a boat in.

For his birthday, Duck got a rod
And a can filled with bait
Which Duck promptly ate.

Duck got a diving board and a slide
And a carrying bag with a towel inside.

And the kind of glasses they advertise
To keep the sun out of duckly eyes.

Duck got a ball that was pumped full of air
And a scuba mask, and a watch to wear

And suntan oil to rub on his beak
So it wouldn't burn and it wouldn't squeak.

Duck looked around and he said, "Thanks a lot!
I'm pleased as can be with the gifts you brought.
But we're far from a lake and far from the sea.
How can I use what you've given to me?"

Everyone laughed, then Hen said, "Just wait!
Your last guest will get here. He's usually late."

They stood around clucking and croaking and such.
Snake hung from a tree, but no one did much.
Toad muttered a bit about lateness and rudeness
Then Hen rolled her eyes. "Here he comes. Well, thank goodness!"

Duck took the package off Tortoise's head.
He shook it and sniffed it and finally said:
"It can't be a river, it can't be a creek.
A river or creek would certainly leak!

"It can't be an ocean, that's too hard to wrap
And there isn't an ocean this small on the map.
It isn't a pond and it isn't a sea.
Whatever this is, it's a real mystery!"

For his birthday, Duck got a plastic pool

That grew and grew as they blew and blew

That held them all as they played and splashed

As they jumped and they dived and they spatter-dashed.

Coming out only for corn crackle cakes
Grasshopper cookies and polliwog shakes.

Giving Duck hugs and squeezing his wing
Crowding around him to cackle and sing:

HAPPY BIRTHDAY TO YOU
HAPPY BIRTHDAY TO YOU

HAPPY BIRTHDAY DEAR DUCK
HAPPY BIRTHDAY TO YOU.

For his birthday Duck got a day filled with friends
Who liked him a lot.
That's what Duck got.